S0-AYY-817

Declan Buhler

MIXED-UP TRUCKS with Baxter, Rosie, and Gus

Copyright © 2016 Green Toys Inc.

Story Concept by Sara Paculdo
Art Direction & Storyboards by Brian Gulassa
Book Design by Iain R. Morris
Produced by Cameron + Company
www.cameronbooks.com

ISBN: 978-0-9971434-2-3
Lot# 1222150509
SKU# BKTK-4342

Printed in the USA

Green Toys Inc.
4000 Bridgeway, Suite 100
Sausalito, CA 94965
www.greentoys.com

MIXED UP TRUCKS

with Baxter, Rosie, and Gus

Written by Robert von Goeben

Illustrated by Nat Iwata

Baxter, Rosie, and Gus are friends,
and have been for a while.

They work together in their trucks,
and they always laugh and smile.

The story begins in the usual way,
when the dogs were little pups.

A time to learn the ins and outs,
along with the downs and ups.

Little Baxter loved to play,
and fetching was his knack.

Whatever you threw, everyone knew,
Baxter would bring it right back.

When Baxter got bigger,
he started to figure,
what he wanted to do.

He drives a dump truck,
fetches the dirt,
and hauls it
back to you.

Rosie, however, loved to dig those
big old holes in the ground.

She'd work her shovel into the dirt,
and oh the stuff she found.

So when she got older, and a little bit bolder,
Rosie knew her spot.

She drives the scooper and digs in the earth,
and loves her job a lot.

And little Gus just chased his tail,
spinning round and round.

He never did catch it, and never got dizzy,
and certainly never fell down.

So when he grew up and went off to work,
Gus really knew his bit.

He's an expert driver of a mixer truck,
it's such a natural fit.

Then one day, they were asked to build a swimming pool deep and long.

But try as they might, it didn't go right;
in fact, it went terribly wrong.

Rosie's job was to dig the hole;
they only needed one.

She did the chore, then dug seven more,
since digging was so much fun.

Baxter's job was very simple,
the dirt needed hauling away.

But he brought it all back,
and filled up the holes,
much to Rosie's dismay.

Gus was in charge of mixing cement,
to pour into the open space.

He was having a blast and mixing too fast,
and cement went all over the place.

Every day, it kept
going this way,
and nothing ever
got done.

The work on the pool was going nowhere, just like it had never begun.

Then one day, they stopped their work,
and decided to have a chat.

They sat on the ground,
and talked till they found,
the problem with
where they were at.

Rosie agreed,
there was only a need,
for one hole rather than eight.

Then Baxter could see,
to let the holes be,
just haul the dirt
and wait.

Gus would fix,
the way that he mixed.
He'd slow down and
not make a mess.

And once they could see,
to work as a team,
they worked with
a lot less stress.

And when then were done,
they had some fun,
swimming in the sunny weather.

And so you see, how good it can be,
when we all just work together.